Taylor Swift Advent Calendar

25 days of surprises,
fun facts and holiday cheer
for Swifties.

Hannah Kurry

Published by

GRAPEVINE BOOKS

www.grapevinebooks.com

email: contact@grapevinebooks.com

Ordering Information:

Quantity sales: Special discounts are

available on quantity purchases

by corporations, associations, and others.

For details, reach out to the publisher.

First published by Grapevine Books, 2025

Contents

Day 1: The Beginning

FUN FACT:

Taylor Swift began writing songs at just 12 years old, creating music that reflected her experiences growing up in Pennsylvania. Her first song, "Lucky You," was about her feelings of being an outsider at school. Although it wasn't released, it marked the beginning of her journey as a singer-songwriter.

Taylor's parents supported her dreams, and they moved to Nashville when she was 14 so she could pursue country music.

ACTIVITY:

Write a short poem/song about your childhood.

Think about a memory that shaped who you are today, whether it's something funny, sad, or special.

JOURNAL:

Write a short poem/song about your childhood, using a strong memory that shaped who you are today.

TRIVIA:

What was the first song Taylor released?

No matter what happens in life, be good to people.

Answer: Tim McGraw

Day 2: Holiday Magic

FUN FACT:

Taylor Swift has always been a big fan of the holiday season. In 2007, she released The Taylor Swift Holiday Collection, a special EP featuring her cover of classic Christmas songs like "Last Christmas" and "Christmases When You Were Mine."

Taylor enjoys the peaceful feeling of Christmas and that she loves the tradition of giving gifts. She also believes the holidays are a time to reflect on everything you're grateful for.

ACTIVITY:

Do a small act of kindness today like surprising someone with a handmade card, or complimenting a stranger. It's never too early to spread joy to those around you!

JOURNAL:

Who do you want to surprise this Christmas and why? Write about how you think they'll react.

TRIVIA:

What classic Christmas song did Taylor cover in her first holiday EP?

You are the best thing that's ever been mine.

Day 3: Debut Era

FUN FACT:

Taylor Swift's debut album Taylor Swift was released in 2006 when she was just 16 years old. The album introduced her unique blend of country and pop music, which was a refreshing sound in the country music scene.

One of the standout tracks, "Tim McGraw," was inspired by Taylor's high school relationships. She wrote the song in her bedroom, and it helped launch her career.

ACTIVITY:

Try to imagine what a Taylor Swift holiday song might sound like: a country ballad, a pop anthem, or a mix of both? Write a few lines of your own holiday-inspired lyrics based on your favorite Taylor song.

TRIVIA:

What's a goal you had when you were 15? How did you work toward it and what did you learn along the way?

JOURNAL:

Which two country legends were mentioned in the album's opening track?

When you think Tim McGraw, I hope you think of me.

Answer: Silent Night

Day 4: Fearless Era

FUN FACT:

Released in 2008, Fearless was Taylor Swift's breakthrough album that solidified her as a superstar. Hits like "Love Story" and "You Belong with Me" became anthems for teens.

Fearless was inspired by Taylor's own high school experiences and the struggles of love and heartbreak. Her honest lyrics resonated with fans and led to her winning numerous awards, including the Grammy for Album of the Year in 2010.

ACTIVITY:

Write down one thing that makes you feel fearless. This could be something big, like standing up for yourself, or something small, like trying something new.

JOURNAL:

Who would you share a dance with no matter what? Describe the moment and the emotions you'd feel.

TRIVIA:

What was Taylor's first Fearless single?

I suffer from girlnextdooritis where the guy is friends with you and that's it.

Answer: Love Story

Day 5: Speak Now Era

FUN FACT:

Taylor Swift wrote all 14 songs on Speak Now, a feat that showcased her songwriting skills. Each song told a story about love, regret, and personal experiences.

The album was a departure from her previous work and was inspired by her experiences of growing up and realizing that not everything is as simple as it seems. One of the most iconic songs on the album is "Dear John," a raw, emotional letter to her former lover, John Mayer.

ACTIVITY:

Try writing a short story about a secret you've never told anyone. Could you turn your secret into a song or poem?

(You don't have to share it with anyone!)

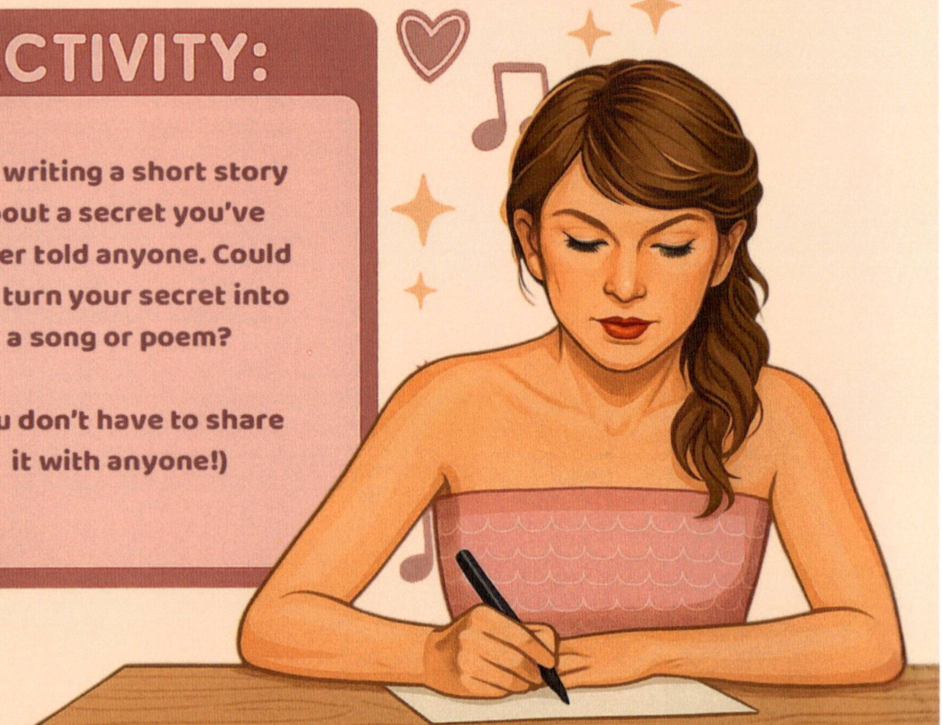

JOURNAL:

What is something you've always wanted to say but haven't yet? Imagine you're writing a letter to them.

TRIVIA:

Which song from Speak Now was meant for Taylor Lautner?

I don't know what I want, so don't ask me.

Answer: Back to December

Day 6: Red Era

FUN FACT:

Red (2012) blends country, pop, and rock, exploring Taylor's heartbreaks and growth. "All Too Well" became iconic, rumored to reference her relationship with Jake Gyllenhaal.

The infamous red scarf in the song is said to be a real-life gift she left behind. Red marked a turning point in her career, showing her willingness to be vulnerable and experiment with musical styles.

ACTIVITY:

Draw a heart using colors that match the emotions of Red. Add a tiny red scarf doodle or lyric inside to capture the story.

JOURNAL:

When was the last time your heart raced with excitement, love, or heartbreak?

TRIVIA:

Which artists featured on the bonus 'The Vault' tracks of Red?

People haven't always been there for me but music always has.

Answer: Phoebe Bridgers and Ed Sheeran

Day 7: 1989 Era

FUN FACT:

1989 (2014) was Taylor's full pop-era debut. The album contains hidden Easter eggs like references to friends like Selena Gomez and Gigi Hadid, and her previous songs.

Fans speculate that "Blank Space" slyly references her dating life. There are also supposed references of her time with Harry Styles in "Out of the Woods" starting with the paper airplane necklace she rips in its music video.

ACTIVITY:

List your top five 1989 songs and write a line about why each feels personal to you.

JOURNAL:

What memories or feelings does 1989 bring up for you?

TRIVIA:

Which 1989 single became a viral music video sensation?

I don't know why, but with you I'd dance in a storm in my best dress.

Answer: Phoebe Bridgers and Ed Sheeran

Day 8: Reputation Era

FUN FACT:

Reputation (2017) explores a darker, edgier side of Taylor. The "snake" persona was inspired by public criticism and feuds, including those with Kanye West and Kim Kardashian.

Her songs subtly nod to these feuds, reclaiming her narrative with clever lyricism and visuals. Hidden Easter eggs reference previous eras, personal relationships, and past controversies.

ACTIVITY:

Write a brief note reflecting on a time you reclaimed your own story or stood up for yourself.

JOURNAL:

When have you had to reinvent yourself and show a new side of who you are?

TRIVIA:

Which Reputation song includes the lyric, "Honey, I rose up from the dead"?

You may think I'm bullet-proof, but I'm not.

Answer: Look what you made me do

Day 9: Lover Era

FUN FACT:

Lover (2019) celebrates joy, romance, and pastel aesthetics. The album is widely believed to be inspired predominantly by Taylor's relationship with Joe Alwyn.

Hidden Easter eggs include nods to the red scarf from Red, her 1989 friends and relationships, and even subtle mentions of Reputation-era drama. The songs highlight activism while being a mosh pit of celebrity appearances right from Katy Perry to RuPaul.

ACTIVITY:

Write a short paragraph about a happy memory or relationship you want to cherish forever.

Draw a small heart or star to symbolize it.

JOURNAL:

What does "forever" mean to you, and which moments in your life feel timeless?

TRIVIA:

Which Lover song celebrates a private, lasting relationship?

The most honest art comes from the middle of the night when nobody is watching.

Answer: Joe Alwyn

Day 10: Folklore Era

FUN FACT:

Folklore (2020) was a surprise pandemic album that tells fictional stories through a calm indie-folk sound. The songs feature Easter eggs, like references to collaborators Aaron Dessner and Jack Antonoff.

The love triangle she wove between the characters James, August, and Betty is central to the storytelling, and attentive fans have found hidden clues in lyric choices and music videos connecting back to other eras.

ACTIVITY:

Write a short folklore-inspired story about a character facing a challenge. Include at least one hidden clue or symbol in your story.

JOURNAL:

When did you first discover a new side of yourself or realize something surprising about your own story?

____

____

____

____

____

____

TRIVIA:

What aesthetic does the folklore album embrace?

____

I'm intimidated by the fear of being average.

Answer: Joe Alwyn

Day 11: Evermore

FUN FACT:

Evermore (2020) is a sister album to Folklore featuring collaborations with Aaron Dessner, Jack Antonoff, and Justin Vernon. It continues her storytelling with characters like Dorothea and Champ.

Taylor's ability to blend real-life experiences with fictional characters is evident in songs like "Champagne Problems," which she co-wrote with Joe Alwyn.

ACTIVITY:

Craft a charm bracelet with nature-inspired charms like leaves, stars, and keys. Use this as a symbolic piece representing the storytelling and themes of Evermore.

JOURNAL:

Describe a time when observing someone else's story made you reflect on your own life.

____

____

____

____

____

____

TRIVIA:

Which Evermore song was a tribute to Taylor's grandmother?

____

Words can break someone, but they can also put them back together

Answer: Marjorie

Day 12: Midnights

FUN FACT:

Midnights (2022) features collaborations with Jack Antonoff, Aaron Dessner, and William Bowery. Fans spotted Easter eggs in the visuals, including lift button numbers and hidden objects referencing prior eras in the Bejewelled and Anti Hero music video.

The album was released with a unique marketing strategy, dropping two versions within hours of each other. "Anti-Hero" became a standout track, with fans linking themes of self-doubt to Taylor's other eras.

ACTIVITY:

Host a late-night listening party with Midnights playing in the background. Turn off the lights and use candles or fairy lights to create a cozy, introspective vibe.

JOURNAL:

Write down three thoughts or emotions that keep you awake. Illustrate one with a small doodle or symbol.

TRIVIA:

Which tracks from Midnights feature hidden references to her Reputation-era themes?

I write about people because I want to understand them and myself better.

Answer: Anti Hero, Vigilante Shit, Karma

Day 13: The Tortured Poets Department

FUN FACT:

The Tortured Poets Department (2024) is believed to be a reference to "The Tortured Man Club," a group chat shared by her ex-boyfriend Joe and his friends.

Taylor Swift revealed the album's existence when she won her 13th Grammy Award for Midnights in February 2024. Her lucky number, 13, played a role: she made the announcement after winning her 13th Grammy, and an "Error 321" message with a faded "13" appeared on her website before the Grammys.

ACTIVITY:

Make a personalized poetry jar filled with your favorite inspirational quotes or song lyrics. Use it for daily reflection and to connect with the introspective mood of the album.

JOURNAL:

Pick a song from TTPD that feels like you. Write your own version of it. Make sure to give it your own spin!

TRIVIA:

Which collaborators helped shape the introspective sound on this album?

Writing can be a mirror, showing you parts of yourself.

Answer: Aaron Dessner and Jack Antonoff

Day 14: The Life of a Showgirl

FUN FACT:

The Life of a Showgirl (2025) features a collaboration with Sabrina Carpenter. Before the release, Taylor created hype by highlighting her engagement to Travis Kelce.

Fans noticed Easter eggs referencing previous tours and eras, including Red and Reputation. Also, if you lined up the titles of all the album tracks, and lined them in the frame's center, the shape of the tracklist makes the same shape as the Eras Tour stage.

ACTIVITY:

Design a custom tour ticket for your dream Taylor Swift concert. Include fun details like the concert date, location, and special performances from your favorite albums.

JOURNAL:

Write about a time when performing publicly revealed a hidden side of you.

TRIVIA:

Which past tour visually referenced Red and Reputation eras with costumes and set design?

I love giving fans little secrets and hidden messages like a treasure hunt.

Answer: The Reputation Stadium Tour

Day 15: Easter Egg Bonanza

FUN FACT:

Taylor Swift is famous for hiding Easter eggs in music videos, album artwork, and social media posts.

Some infamous easter eggs include the incorporation of her cats, particularly Benjamin Button in the "ME!" music video. Her highly detailed and complex clues, like the "Et Tu, Brute?" inscriptions on a throne in the "The Fate of Ophelia" video alluding to betrayal and the "Take 100" on a clapboard referencing Travis Kelce's number 87 are the most recent additions.

ACTIVITY:

Create your own Easter egg.

Hide a symbol, lyric, or drawing for someone to discover.

JOURNAL:

Have you ever left a secret message for someone to discover later? What was the message and how did it feel?

TRIVIA:

Which Red prop became a recurring Easter egg in later albums?

Songwriting is my therapy, it's how I cope with things.

Answer: The Red Scarf

Day 16: Fashion and Iconic Looks

FUN FACT:

Taylor Swift is known for her ever-evolving fashion sense, from country girl chic in her early years to bold, metallic-inspired couture on her later tours. Her iconic looks, like the red lipstick and striped dresses from 1989, the glittery bodysuits from Lover, and the vintage-inspired outfits from Folklore, reflect her bold personality and artistic growth.

Her outfits often convey emotional depth and are an extension of the stories she tells in her songs.

ACTIVITY:

Create a style board using pictures or magazine clippings that reflect your personal fashion icon. Try to channel Taylor's bold, vintage, or whimsical looks from any of her eras.

JOURNAL:

What's one piece of clothing or an accessory that makes you feel empowered or confident? Describe why it holds significance for you.

____

____

____

____

____

____

TRIVIA:

Which album featured a major fashion shift with bold, high-fashion looks?

____

Fashion is the armor to survive the reality of everyday life.

Answer: 1989

Day 17: Lyrics Deep Dive

FUN FACT:

Taylor Swift's songwriting is known for its emotional depth, vivid imagery, and storytelling ability. Many fans have noticed that her lyrics often contain hidden messages and Easter eggs.

Songs like "All Too Well" and "Invisible String" have sparked intense fan analysis, with listeners uncovering meanings tied to Taylor's personal life. Blending personal stories with universal themes has made her lyrics relatable to millions.

ACTIVITY:

Pick one of your favorite Taylor Swift songs and analyze the lyrics in-depth. Create a visual representation (drawing, mood board, or color palette) that captures the emotions the song evokes.

JOURNAL:

Which lyric or song from Taylor's discography resonates with you the most, and why? How does it make you feel when you listen to it?

TRIVIA:

Which Speak Now song is dedicated to Taylor Swift's fans?

Every show is a chance to tell a story, whether it's mine or someone else's.

Answer: Long Live

Day 18: Taylor and Her Cats

FUN FACT:

Taylor Swift's love for her cats, Meredith, Olivia, and Benjamin, has been well-documented in her social media posts and interviews. Her cats have become internet celebrities in their own right, often featured in her music videos and on her Instagram.

Taylor has said that they provide her with emotional comfort, especially during hard times. Their personalities often shine through in her music, and their names have interesting origin stories.

ACTIVITY:

Create a fun cat-themed craft (like a drawing, DIY cat bookmark, or cat-themed accessories) inspired by Taylor's love for her feline friends.

JOURNAL:

Do you have a pet that brings you comfort and joy? Write about your bond and how they make you feel.

TRIVIA:

Which cat is named after the protagonist in the show Grey's Anatomy?

Cats are independent and loyal, and I love that about them.

Answer: Meredith

Day 19: Music Video Moments

FUN FACT:

Taylor Swift's music videos are known for their stunning visuals and intricate storytelling. Videos like "Bad Blood" and "You Belong With Me" feature cinematic narratives, while others like "Delicate" play with creative symbolism.

Taylor's ability to use music videos as an extension of her albums has allowed fans to dive deeper into her artistry, with every detail holding meaning, from outfits to settings.

ACTIVITY:

Choose one of Taylor's iconic music videos and recreate a scene that stands out to you. It could be a costume, a pose, or a setting. Capture the emotion of the video through your own creative interpretation.

JOURNAL:

Which Taylor Swift music video speaks to you the most and why? How does it visually enhance the connection?

____

____

____

____

____

____

TRIVIA:

Which Taylor Swift music video featured Gigi Hadid?

____

Music videos are like short films for me. I want them to tell a story.

Answer: Bad Blood

Day 20: Awards and Milestones

FUN FACT:

Taylor Swift has accumulated an impressive number of awards, including 11 Grammy Awards and over 40 Billboard Music Awards. She was the first woman to win the Grammy for Album of the Year four times, with Fearless, 1989, Folklore and Midnights.

Throughout her career, Taylor broke records and impacted pop culture, including becoming the first artist in history to simultaneously occupy all top 10 spots on the Billboard Hot 100.

ACTIVITY:

Create a mini trophy or award that represents a personal achievement or goal of yours. Decorate it with items or colors that symbolize success in your life.

Answer: Tim McGraw

JOURNAL:

What personal achievement are you most proud of? Write about the journey it took to reach that milestone and how it made you feel.

TRIVIA:

Which Swift song is the longest-charting song by a female artist in the history of the Billboard Hot 100?

Success is not about the awards you get, but about how many people you inspire.

Answer: All Too Well (10-Minute Version)

Day 21: Bookworm Side

FUN FACT:

Taylor Swift is an avid reader, with a deep love for novels, poetry, and even classic literature. She has mentioned books that have influenced her songwriting like The Great Gatsby and The Bell Jar.

Many of her songs, like "Betty" and "August," reflect the themes of coming-of-age novels and the emotional depth found in literature. She often refers to books as a way to fuel her creativity and to understand complex human emotions.

ACTIVITY:

Pick up a favorite book or a new one and create a book-inspired playlist. Choose songs that fit the vibe of the book, whether it's love, heartbreak, or adventure.

JOURNAL:

What book has had the biggest impact on your life, and why? What lessons or emotions did it bring you?

____

____

____

____

____

____

TRIVIA:

Which book did Taylor say inspired her song "Betty"?

____

Writing a song is like telling a story through music.

Answer: The Great Gatsby

Day 22: Songwriting Secrets

FUN FACT:

Taylor Swift has always been open about her songwriting process, which is often inspired by her personal experiences and emotions. She has a habit of carrying a notebook everywhere to jot down lyrics, ideas, or thoughts that come to her at any given time.

Taylor also often experiments with song structures, using unexpected chord progressions. Her ability to tell vivid, often cinematic stories through her lyrics is why her songs resonate so deeply with listeners.

ACTIVITY:

Write down three words that describe your current emotions. Use those words as inspiration to create a short melody or lyrical phrase. Experiment with different rhythms and melodies.

JOURNAL:

How does writing or creating art help you express emotions or thoughts that you can't easily say out loud?

____

____

____

____

____

____

TRIVIA:

Which song did Taylor write in just 20 minutes?

____

Books are the ultimate escape. You live inside another world and understand life through different eyes.

Answer: You Belong With Me

Day 23: Swiftie Slang

FUN FACT:

Swifties have created their own unique slang and traditions, often drawn from Taylor's lyrics and social media posts. Terms like "Taylurking," referring to Taylor secretly reading fan comments online, and "Easter eggs," referring to hidden clues in her music and videos, are commonly used within the fanbase.

Swifties also celebrate release parties, album release countdowns, and special holidays like "Swiftmas" as a way to connect and celebrate Taylor's music.

ACTIVITY:

Host a Swiftie trivia night with friends or fellow fans. Include questions about Taylor's music, lyrics, and career milestones. Create a prize for the winner, such as a Taylor Swift-inspired accessory or themed playlist.

JOURNAL:

What Swiftie tradition or slang term do you connect with the most? Why do you think it resonates with you or your experience as a fan?

____

____

____

____

____

____

TRIVIA:

What is the term to describe the small hidden clues Taylor includes in her music videos?

____

Swifties are like family, supporting each other and celebrating every moment.

Answer: Easter eggs

Day 24: Eras Highlights

FUN FACT:

Taylor's Eras Tour was a celebration of her entire career, spanning all of her albums. The tour featured iconic costumes and set designs inspired by each era of her music, from the country roots of Fearless to the indie-folk vibes of her sister albums.

Fans loved the surprise songs that Taylor performed at each concert, creating unforgettable experiences. The Eras Tour is one of the most successful tours of all time, both critically and commercially.

ACTIVITY:

Create a concert poster for your own Eras Tour, featuring all of Taylor's albums and the iconic looks you'd want to see live. Add elements from each era's visuals and themes to make it a true fan experience.

JOURNAL:

If you could attend any concert on Taylor's Eras Tour, what song or moment are you most excited to experience?

____

____

____

____

____

____

TRIVIA:

Which surprise song from Folklore was performed for the first time ever during the Eras Tour?

____

Just be yourself, there is no one better.

Answer: Betty

Day 25: Merry Swiftmas Finale

FUN FACT:

The Swiftie community is an incredibly loyal and supportive fan base, especially during the holiday season. From holiday-themed fan meetups to Swiftmas gift exchanges, Swifties create their own unique traditions that reflect the joy and love they share for Taylor.

Taylor called Swifties her "family" and celebrating their kindness and unity, especially when it comes to spreading holiday cheer and supporting each other.

ACTIVITY:

Create a Swiftie Christmas ornament to celebrate the holidays. Use your favorite Taylor lyric or album cover design as inspiration to decorate it. Hang it on your tree as a reminder of your connection with the Swiftie family.

JOURNAL:

Write about a special tradition you share with fellow Swifties that brings joy during this festive time of year.

TRIVIA:

What special live event did Taylor host for her fans in 2020, giving them the first taste of the Folklore album?

My fans are the longest and best relationship I've ever had.

Answer: Folklore Secret Sessions

Swiftie Holiday Checklist

- [ ] Day 1: Write a letter to your favorite era. Tell "1989" or "Folklore" what it means to you.
- [ ] Day 2: Bake a batch of cookies inspired by Lover (for instance, use pastel sprinkles and heart shapes.)
- [ ] Day 3: Create your own friendship bracelet with lyrics from your favorite song.
- [ ] Day 4: Have a "Red" night, wear something cozy and red while listening to the album.
- [ ] Day 5: Make a gratitude list of five things Taylor's music has taught you.
- [ ] Day 6: Decorate your room with fairy lights and call it your "Midnights" glow-up.
- [ ] Day 7: Listen to "Christmas Tree Farm" while sipping hot cocoa.
- [ ] Day 8: Write your own song or poem about winter memories.
- [ ] Day 9: Create a mini vision board for the new year inspired by "New Year's Day."
- [ ] Day 10: Watch a Taylor concert film or live performance online.
- [ ] Day 11: Recreate one of Taylor's iconic looks using what's already in your closet.
- [ ] Day 12: Draw or paint your favorite Taylor album cover.

- [ ] **Day 13: Celebrate 13 Day!—make a wish and do one kind thing for someone else.**
- [ ] **Day 14: Host a mini listening party for your favorite album with friends or family.**
- [ ] **Day 15: Write a thank-you note to a friend who's been there for you "through the eras."**
- [ ] **Day 16: Take a peaceful walk while listening to Evermore and notice the winter details.**
- [ ] **Day 17: Learn a fun Taylor lyric by heart and record yourself performing it.**
- [ ] **Day 18: Have a cozy pajama movie night with Cats or Valentine's Day.**
- [ ] **Day 19: Make or print holiday cards using Taylor-inspired quotes.**
- [ ] **Day 20: Reorganize your playlist by mood.**
- [ ] **Day 21: Read a book Taylor has mentioned loving, such as The Great Gatsby or To Kill a Mockingbird.**
- [ ] **Day 22: Design your own Taylor-themed holiday ornament.**
- [ ] **Day 23: Write a short story inspired by one of her songs, either realistic or fantasy or something in between!**
- [ ] **Day 24: Record a short message to your future self about what this year meant to you.**
- [ ] **Day 25: Open your favorite Taylor memory. Watch a clip, reread lyrics, or sing along one more time**

Color It Out

Create Your Own Taylor-Inspired Lyrics
Guided template for writing your own song or poem

Swift Holiday Playlist

NEW YEAR'S DAY

In my heart is a Christmas tree farm

Where the people would come

To dance under sparkling lights

And I just wanna be there tonight

CHRISTMAS MUST BE SOMETHING MORE

You'd see that today holds
something special

Something holy, not superficial

So here's something you
should know that is for sure

Christmas must be something more

CHRISTMAS TREE FARM

In my heart is a Christmas tree farm

Where the people would come

To dance under sparkling lights

And I just wanna be there tonight

FOREVER WINTER

I'd fall to pieces on the floor

If you weren't around

Too young to know it gets better

I'll be summer sun for you forever

Forever winter if you go

THE MOMENT I KNEW

They're all laughing
As I'm looking around the room
But there was one thing missing
And that was the moment I knew

'TIS THE DAMN SEASON

We could call it even

Even though I'm leavin'

And I'll be yours for the weekend

'Tis the damn season

Create Your Own Inspired Lyrics

What your song or poem be about? Love, friendship, self-discovery, or growing up? Think about a moment you want to capture.

Every Taylor song tells a story. Write down who your story is about (you, a friend, or a character), what happens, and three key emotions.

Think of one powerful line that sums up your message. This will be your chorus or repeating line. Make it emotional, honest, and easy to remember.

Start shaping your story into short verses. Use imagery and details (like a red scarf, a city street, or a coffee cup) to make your words come alive.

Read your lyrics aloud. Do they sound smooth or clunky? Adjust the lines until they flow naturally like a melody.

Choose a title that feels poetic or symbolic, something that captures the heart of your song in just a few words.

Printed in Great Britain
by Amazon

40c410a0-7aaa-4736-8cd7-c82f3a97b4d0R01